Acting Edition

The Glorious World of Crowns, Kinks and Curls

by Keli Goff

I0591825

‖ SAMUEL FRENCH ‖

FOR PRODUCTION INQUIRIES

UNITED STATES AND CANADA
info@concordtheatricals.com
1-866-979-0447

UNITED KINGDOM AND EUROPE
licensing@concordtheatricals.co.uk
020-7054-7298

Each title is subject to availability from Concord Theatricals Corp.,
depending upon country of performance. Please be aware that THE
GLORIOUS WORLD OF CROWNS, KINKS AND CURLS may not be
licensed by Concord Theatricals Corp. in your territory. Professional
and amateur producers should contact the nearest Concord Theatricals
Corp. office or licensing partner to verify availability.

No one shall make any changes in this title(s) for the purpose of production. No part of this book may be reproduced, stored in a retrieval system, scanned, uploaded, or transmitted in any form, by any means, now known or yet to be invented, including mechanical, electronic, digital, photocopying, recording, videotaping, or otherwise, without the prior written permission of the publisher. No one shall share this title(s), or any part of this title(s), through any social media or file hosting websites.

For all inquiries regarding motion picture, television, online/digital and other media rights, please contact Concord Theatricals Corp.

MUSIC AND THIRD-PARTY MATERIALS USE NOTE

Licensees are solely responsible for obtaining formal written permission from copyright owners to use copyrighted music and/or other copyrighted third-party materials (e.g., artworks, logos) in the performance of this play and are strongly cautioned to do so. If no such permission is obtained by the licensee, then the licensee must use only original music and materials that the licensee owns and controls. Licensees are solely responsible and liable for clearances of all third-party copyrighted materials, including without limitation music, and shall indemnify the copyright owners of the play(s) and their licensing agent, Concord Theatricals Corp., against any costs, expenses, losses and liabilities arising from the use of such copyrighted third-party materials by licensees. For music, please contact the appropriate music licensing authority in your territory for the rights to any incidental music.

IMPORTANT BILLING AND CREDIT REQUIREMENTS

If you have obtained performance rights to this title, please refer to your licensing agreement for important billing and credit requirements.

THE GLORIOUS WORLD OF CROWNS, KINKS AND CURLS was first produced by the Baltimore Center Stage, streaming from March 25th to May 2nd, 2021. The performance was directed by Bianca LaVerne Jones, with scenic and costume design by Dede Ayite, hair and wig design by Nikiya Mathis, lighting design by Stacey Derosier, and sound design by Twi McCallum. The Stage Manager was Danielle Teague-Daniels. The cast was as follows:

LADY 1 . . . . .Stori Ayers

LADY 2 . . . . .Awa Sal Secka

LADY 3 . . . . Shayna Small

CHARACTERS

LADY 1 – A Black woman
LADY 2 – A Black woman
LADY 3 – A Black woman

AUTHOR'S NOTES

In the tradition of *For Colored Girls*...and *The Vagina Monologues*, *The Glorious World of Crowns, Kinks and Curls* is a collection of monologues, scenes and poetry, featuring voices of Black women from around the globe recalling unforgettable moments in their lives in which their hair – and their complicated relationships with their hair – took center stage. From afros to braids, and weddings to funerals, *The Glorious World of Crowns, Kinks and Curls,* will take audiences on an intimate and unparalleled journey into the world of Black womanhood.

While ideally at least one of the **LADIES** should identify as curvy, please note that each cast member, regardless of her actual appearance, will play a multitude of women and girls of different ages, skin tones and hair textures, representing a diverse spectrum of Black women. Please also note that the ladies of the cast can play whichever characters make the most sense for that particular production at that particular time, except in those instances in which a **LADY**'s number is specified for continuity and clarity.

*(As audience members enter the theater, they hear the following audio on an ongoing loop, until lights come up. **This audio marks the official start of the play and is an essential part of establishing the setting.** [The audio can either be prerecorded or can be recreated by cast members offstage using microphones or just their voices.] The audio, in no particular order, includes:*

• *Sounds of blow dryers which can be heard blowing for a bit, followed by...*

• *A woman's voice saying: "that's too hot..."*

• *And another replying: "Do you want it dry or not? You said you didn't have time to sit under."*

• *A "sizzling" sound – to signify a hot pressing comb, followed by...*

• *A woman's voice shouting: "Ow! You burned me!"*

• *And another replying: "I wouldn't have if you would sit still! I'm trying to get your edges."*

• *Sounds of hair being cut. Followed by...*

• *A woman's voice saying: "Not too short!"*

• *Another woman then says: "I'm burning. When can you rinse it off?"*

- *And another replies: "It hasn't been on long enough. Your hair's not straight yet."*

- *Another woman saying: "Honey. I'm a hairstylist not a magician. I can give you Janet Jackson's hair but I can't make you look like her. No one can."*

- *Laughter. Lots and lots of laughter – loud, contagious, belly-busting laughter from women.*

Please note, that music with a gospel or R&B feel can also be played intermittently* as audience members file in so that the audio doesn't begin to feel repetitive as it plays. As the lights go down, everyone in the audience will listen to the entire audio above in full, together, side by side. This is the first true scene of the play.

Once this setting – this feeling of being inside of a Black women's hair salon – is firmly established, then the lights come up.)

---

* A license to produce THE GLORIOUS WORLD OF CROWNS, KINKS AND CURLS does not include a performance license for any third-party or copyrighted music. Licensees should create an original composition or use music in the public domain. For further information, please see Music Use Note on page 3.

1. Welcome/The Audition

(We see one Black woman standing on stage. She begins speaking directly to the audience.)

ACTRESS. WELCOME!!!

How ya'll doing?

(Wait for audience response.)

Well, we're so glad you're here, for an evening of laughter and maybe even a few tears. Basically you paid for a theater ticket, but you may actually leave feeling like you spent a couple of hours with some really FUN, really funny, really engaging and really non-judgmental therapists.

We hope that when you leave you will feel as though you've spent the afternoon, or evening as the case may be, with old friends.

Or maybe you'll feel like you made some new ones.

Maybe a story will remind you of your mother or your sister. Maybe a story will remind you of the woman you once were, or the woman you hope to be. Or maybe even the woman you once hoped you COULD be.

(Pause.)

But most of all we hope that when you leave here you will know that regardless of all of the people out there whose only job seems to be trying to make us all feel insecure about who we are, you will know that you should hold your head high.

Not just because of who you are, but because of every little girl who *sees you for who you are*.

Think of your strength – your confidence – your pride, as your superpowers. Superpowers more powerful, more magical than ANY cape or kryptonite, because they can save other women and girls just by showing them that they have a right to exist and BE SEEN... in a world that often treats us as invisible. If YOU have the courage to walk tall in a world that tries to make you feel small – then maybe other women and little girls will feel like they can too.

(Pause.)

So ENJOY!

Thank you.

(Pause.)

(A voice booms from the back of the theater. It's another lady. We hear her but do not see her during the course of this scene.)

CASTING DIRECTOR. Thank you!

That was great. That was really, really great. Moving.

Oh I see here you studied at Juilliard? What have you been doing since you graduated?

ACTRESS. A few readings... and uh... a commercial... a national commercial.

CASTING DIRECTOR. Oh yeah... I see that here. *(Pause.)*

I love Playtex tampons, by the way. They really are great.

ACTRESS. Yeah. They are. *(Pause.)*

That was actually my line in the commercial.

"You can count on Playtex. They really are great."

CASTING DIRECTOR. Well thanks for coming in.

ACTRESS. Thank you. *(She turns to go, then turns back.)*

Look, the truth is I've mainly been waiting tables since I graduated and when my agent told me that you all were turning the book *Scars* into a play I told him to do whatever it takes to get me an audition. Because even if you don't have physical scars all of us have scars of some kind that we carry around with us, and within us. I've struggled with my weight and body image stuff for years and well... I just know what it's like to walk through the world and have people not see you but look right through you.

And the stories in this play are fundamentally about women wanting to be seen for who they are. Not dehumanized for who they are OR judged for who we are... and how we look. I mean *they*... how they look.

So that's all to say that I would do anything to get this part. *(Pause... catching how that sounds.)*

Well not ANYTHING... but you know... within reason...

(Pause.) And I'm not just saying that because I have less than two hundred dollars left in my bank account and they just cut my cable off...

> *(Pause. We hear the* **CASTING DIRECTOR** *laugh.)*

CASTING DIRECTOR. Okay. I'll pass that on.

Thanks for coming in.

ACTRESS. Thanks for seeing me.

> *(She turns to go.)*

CASTING DIRECTOR. Oh – one more thing. Your hair is adorable. What's that style called? It's not an afro exactly...

ACTRESS. Well it's natural. It's my natural curls...

CASTING DIRECTOR. "Natural"? Huh. Well, it's super cute.

ACTRESS. Thanks...

CASTING DIRECTOR. But I know they're doing a really stripped down production. They want all of the actresses to look as... well, *natural* as possible, so that means no wigs or anything. So would it be possible for you to change your hair?

ACTRESS. Ummm... change it how?

CASTING DIRECTOR. Well I don't really know much about YOUR kind of hair.

But I do know that they all like Michelle Obama. I mean all of the producers just donated to her husband's campaign so if you made your hair look more like hers, you'd be gold.

ACTRESS. Michelle Obama?

CASTING DIRECTOR. Yeah. Don't you just love her?

ACTRESS. Well of course... But...

CASTING DIRECTOR. So if you could just change your hair to how she wears hers, or you know how other professional-looking Black women wear theirs. You know, ladylike. Not an afro or braids... or natural or whatever, just nice and ladylike.

ACTRESS. Uh... so you want me to chemically straighten my hair?

CASTING DIRECTOR. I don't actually know what that means. But I DO know our producers are older and more traditional... you're just so talented. I'd hate for something as silly as how you CHOOSE to wear your hair to hurt your chances. *(Pause.)*

I mean this show could change your whole life. And after all, it's just hair.

(There is a palpable silence.)

ACTRESS. Um...um...

(Lights out.)

2. Everybody Has a Story

*(When the lights come up the **ACTRESS** steps forward as one of the **LADIES** in this scene and the **CASTING DIRECTOR** emerges from the audience to join as well, while the other **LADY** emerges from the wings...)*

LADY 1. Everybody has a story.

LADY 3. EVERYBODY!

LADY 2. Everybody!

Why is hair so, so...

LADY 3. ...much drama?

LADY 2. Yeah... and why is it such a source of... of...

LADY 1. Frustration?

LADY 3. Pain?

LADY 2. Heartache.

(The next two lines are delivered rapid fire...)

LADY 1. My grandmother used to call her hair her crown and glory...

LADY 2. My grandmother said I would have been pretty if my hair wasn't so NAPPY.

(This one is delivered slower...)

LADY 3. My great grandmother said the only reason her hair was straight was because the slaveowner who owned our family had raped her grandmother. So she LOVED that all of her great granddaughters had REALLY nappy hair.

(They all take a moment to take this statement in and to look at each other and the audience.)

LADY 1. Whether you have kinks...

LADY 2. Or curls...

LADY 3. Whether you're rich...

LADY 1. Or poor...

LADY 2. Thin...

LADY 3. Or thick...

LADY 1. Whether you have LOTS of hair...

LADY 2. Or none at all...

LADY 3. We ALL ...

(They all look at each other.)

LADY 1, LADY 2 & LADY 3. Have a story about our crown and GLORY ...

(Lights down.)

3. Don't Touch!

(This scene is intended to clearly affirm the ensemble nature of this piece. As such the delivery should feel like a fast-paced conversation between sisters who have told each other the same story so many times they deliver the lines almost in harmony like a trio singing one song.)

LADY 1. I had just started a new office job.

LADY 2. I was meeting my roommate's parents for the first time.

LADY 3. It was our first date.

LADY 1. "Good afternoon Wheeler & Keeler, how may I help you?"

LADY 2. I was the first person in my family to go to college, scholarship, of course. My roommate's grandfather had been President of the college and her great-grandfather had been Vice President... of the United States.

LADY 3. I met him on Raya, it's supposed to be a dating app for super successful people. I'd tried Tinder, I'd tried Bumble, I'd tried Match and so far I'd ended up with no engagement ring but two STIs and a restraining order.

LADY 1. I'd graduated top of my class at secretarial school. I was told Wheeler & Keeler was a great place to work. The executives there were supposed to be real decent. And some of them were also supposed to be REAL single... *(She smiles.)*

LADY 2. My roommate, was very tall, very thin, very blonde, VERY rich and VERY WOKE. If Wokeness Performance Art were a Major she would have graduated with honors. The first thing she did was introduce herself. The second thing she did was apologize for her privilege. The third thing she did was give me a hug and then she burst into tears. It was... weird.

LADY 3. I'd never heard of him but apparently he was a successful hip-hop producer. He said he'd discovered his connection to the raw, emotional power of Black music when the teen rap group Kriss Kross performed their hit, *Jump* at his Bar Mitzvah.

(*Pause.*)

I could tell it was going to be a LONG night.

LADY 1. Everything was going pretty well. Everyone at the office seemed to like me.

LADY 2. I could tell my roommate liked me.

She told me that my essence reminded her of her favorite celebrity: Nina Simone... which was kind of odd because I don't sing and I'm biracial so I don't really look like Nina Simone at all. So it was... weird.

LADY 3. He told me he considered Billie Holliday the sexiest woman who ever walked the planet. And he considered her rendition of Strange Fruit the sexiest recording ever made.

I asked him he if realized the song was about lynching.

LADY 1. The only female executive at the office was a bigshot who went to Harvard or somewhere, but she made a point of inviting all of the assistants to lunch, which was really nice of her. Like a mentoring thing.

LADY 2. So even though she was a little weird... she was harmless and tried REALLY hard, so when she invited me to spend Thanksgiving with her family... I thought about it and I was seeing my family over Christmas anyway, and well... my roommate's family was spending Thanksgiving on their yacht... in the Caribbean. So... (*She smiles.*)

LADY 3. I knew there wouldn't be a second date. Nice guy, zero chemistry. And it's not because he's white. I'd dated white before. I'd dated Black before. I'd dated brown before. At this point I was willing to try dating someone blue. I just wanted a nice, normal guy that I vibe with. Hell, at this point I'd settle for a little chemistry and good credit.

LADY 1. It was at lunch that it happened...

LADY 2. It was actually during Thanksgiving dinner that it happened...

LADY 3. We had just ordered dessert when it happened...

LADY 1. The fancy lady executive told me she loved my look...

LADY 2. Her mother told me I was so pretty...

LADY 3. He told me I was beautiful...

(All three begin to speak in unison.)

LADY 1. And then she told me she loved my hair.

LADY 2. And then she told me she loved my hair.

LADY 3. And then he told me he loved my hair.

LADY 1. And then I saw it...

LADY 2. And then I saw it...

LADY 3. And then I saw it...

(They all reach out with their hands.)

LADY 1. The hand!!!!

LADY 2. The hand!!!

LADY 3. The hand!!!

(They stop speaking in unison.)

LADY 1. She touched my hair.

LADY 2. She actually touched my hair!

LADY 3. He reached over to touch my hair.

LADY 1. She said "It just looks so fun to touch, I couldn't resist!"

LADY 2. When I saw her hand coming, I didn't know what to do. I mean, I'm on her yacht for crying out loud. She's feeding me Thanksgiving dinner, I didn't want to be rude, but petting someone's hair like they're an animal IS RUDE!

LADY 3. When his hand got near my face... I didn't even know what was happening... what I was doing. It was like a Karate Kid style reflex. You know wax-on/wax-off *(She does the hand motion of waxing on a window from the* Karate Kid *movie.)*

LADY 1. I was shocked. And PISSED. She's an educated woman... She went to Harvard or somewhere, for crying out loud, she should know better!

LADY 2. These are rich people... they should know better.

LADY 3. He's a hip-hop producer. He's been around enough Black women. He should know better!

> *(Pause. They all stand in a powerful silence. And then...)*

LADY 3. Well if he didn't know before. He knows now. Because unfortunately when I made my wax-on/wax-off motion my hand accidentally made contact with his nose, and well... broke it.

> *(Pause.)*

LADY 2. She felt up my hair like we were on a first date.

I was humiliated and irritated. And had nowhere to go... the downside of being on a luxury yacht.

LADY 1. I didn't say anything... at first. I'm just a receptionist and she's an executive and I... was embarrassed.

LADY 2. I knew I should say something, but I also knew if I did I would be considered the poor little Black girl they treated to an extravagant vacation who then showed her gratitude by insinuating they're racist. I didn't know what to do...

LADY 3. I offered to pay for dinner. I didn't know what else to do...

LADY 1. And then I decided what to do. After she petted my hair, everyone continued eating, like nothing was wrong. And I realized that's the problem. No one at that table realized what she did to me was rude and wrong. So I waited until we were right in the middle of a good conversation. Everyone was laughing and then I stood up walked over to the fancy lady executive and began petting HER hair.

> *(The actor begins miming feeling up someone else's scalp.)*

I said, "You know, your hair feels really interesting. So different. What do you use on it?" She looked real confused and then kind of terrified and then just mumbled something about shampoo. I just grinned and then I sat back down and continued eating as if nothing had happened.

LADY 2. And then I decided to kill them... with kindness. *(She smiles.)*

After my roommate's mom finished groping my hair and telling me how "interesting" it felt, I stood up and announced that everyone was welcome to walk by my chair and pet my head since I'd noticed that Caucasian people loved doing that so much. I then said if it would be more convenient, I would be willing to walk by every single chair and lean over so they could feel my hair without leaving the comfort of their seats.

LADY 1. She avoided me in the hallway every time she saw me after that. But one of the other assistants emailed me later to tell me that I was a "bad ass" for standing up for myself. The two of us went to lunch the next day and ended up becoming best friends.

LADY 2. My roommate's mother turned bright red, and then asked her dad to carve the turkey but then my roommate did something else: she laughed. Then she asked if I wanted to pet *her* hair to make up for her mom petting mine. I realized in that moment that my roommate may have been cooler than I'd given her credit for. I mean, her mother didn't laugh and I knew that would be my last time on their yacht. But I didn't care, because I also knew it would be *her* last time petting a Black woman's head like a puppy.

LADY 3. I took him to the hospital. And then something strange happened. He told me it was the most interesting first date he'd ever been on, and asked me for a second. The truth is, I wasn't that into him, but the fact that he had such a sense of humor about the whole thing... well I figured why not... but I made him promise me one thing...

LADY 1. PLEASE promise me one thing...

LADY 2. I hope you will **all** promise me one thing.

(They all speak in unison.)

LADY 1. DON'T EVER TOUCH A BLACK WOMAN'S HAIR WITHOUT HER PERMISSION.

LADY 2. DON'T EVER TOUCH A BLACK WOMAN'S HAIR WITHOUT HER PERMISSION.

LADY 3. DON'T EVER TOUCH A BLACK WOMAN'S HAIR WITHOUT HER PERMISSION.

(Lights down.)

4. Dear God, It's Me, Amaya

(When lights come up the year 1995 should be visible somewhere on the stage. This scene can either be delivered via audio, previously recorded by an actor [with accompanying imagery that conveys Black girlhood, such as the silhouette of a child] or the piece can be performed by an adult actor channeling a child.)

AMAYA. Dear God...

This is Amaya... but you know that already because mommy says you know... everything.

Which means... you know that I actually DID DO the thing yesterday that I told mommy I didn't do.

And I know I'm not supposed to lie... so... sorry about that. But I only lied because she said if I get into trouble one more time this week I can't go to Samantha's sleepover. And since you know EVERYTHING God, I know, YOU KNOW that's not fair.

So... I'm praying to say sorry I didn't tell mommy the truth...

And I'm also praying because it's my birthday soon. I'll be eight.

I know you already know that... but I'm just reminding you, because there's a list of presents I want and I know there are lots of kids in the world who have birthdays you have to remember and I know I mentioned this yesterday but just in case you forgot: I really want a dog. I'll settle for a new bicycle but I really want a dog.

In Sunday school we learned that it's important to pray for others, not just for ourselves. So I am praying to ask that you bless Samantha with tickets to see N'Sync for HER birthday...

(Pause.)

So that I can go see them with her.

I also wanted to pray and ask that you bless Sherry at her audition this weekend so that she gets the part she wants on *Sister, Sister*...

(Pause.)

So that I can go with her and meet Tia and Tamera.

I also hope you will bring my daddy home safe. I know what he's doing's important. Mommy says he's a hero who saves people and that's why he's away so much.

But I already knew that. Daddy's always been MY hero.

He SAVES ME from getting in trouble with mommy all the time.

Mommy says daddy lets me get away with murder which is NOT true.

I've NEVER murdered anyone.

See mommies lie sometimes too.

Speaking of murder, I know I'm not allowed to ask you to kill anyone God, but Tommy Smith has been really mean. He put gum in my hair. He got in trouble for it but I don't think he got in enough trouble. See mommy had to cut the gum out of my hair and now I look like a boy. Or more like a boy. The other girls at school have pretty hair and I don't. I know I don't because none of the boys say I have pretty hair. Tyrone and Jerome are the only boys in my class who look like me and Sherry is the only girl who looks like me. But her mom is white so Sherry has long hair with big curls. So I was wondering if it wouldn't be too much trouble and you're not too busy, could you please bless me with pretty hair? That would be the best birthday present ever... even better than a dog.

(Pause.)

I mean I still want the dog... I'm just saying long hair would be nice too.

It doesn't have to be super long. I just wish it weren't so... well Tyrone said I was nappy-headed. I don't want to be nappy-headed. I'm already dark brown. Which mommy says makes me pretty like chocolate, but if I had long hair, then maybe others would consider me pretty not just my mommy. But Tyrone said I'm dark AND nappy-headed. And the way he said it, I know it's a bad thing. So if I have to stay dark could you maybe make me less nappy-headed? If you could do this one thing for me... I'll be an extra good girl from now on. I just want... I just want to be pretty... like Tia and Tamera.

(Another voice – **HER MOTHER** *shouts from offstage.)*

HER MOTHER. Amaya! Time to go.

AMAYA. Be right there mommy!

Oh and God, one more thing, please make sure mommy never, EVER finds out what I did yesterday because if she does I'll be in REALLY BIG trouble.

HER MOTHER. Amaya!

AMAYA. Thanks for listening God!

HER MOTHER. AMAYA!!!!

AMAYA. Amen!

5. Gabrielle and the Wedding

*(A **LADY** stands on the stage and either her costume or the set décor denote a wedding. She can either be preparing to walk down the aisle for her own, or attending another, while reminiscing.)*

MOTHER'S VOICE OFFSTAGE. OH. MY. GOD.

GABRIELLE. Those were the three words my mother greeted me with when she finally saw me just before I walked down the aisle to marry the love of my life.

MOTHER'S VOICE OFFSTAGE. Oh. My. God.

GABRIELLE. She said it again. Which was a bit of a surprise because we were in a church and mom's REALLY religious and rarely takes the Lord's name in vain. But it was a big day and big moment so she said it once more – this time with feeling...

MOTHER'S VOICE OFFSTAGE. OH MY GOD!

GABRIELLE. She then began to cry.

(Pause.)

But not tears of joy, as so many mothers and fathers do on their daughter's wedding day.

They were tears of... tears of... well, I'll let the next words that came out of her mouth explain:

MOTHER'S VOICE OFFSTAGE. WHAT DID YOU DO TO YOUR HAIR??????

GABRIELLE. See I had decided to change my hair right before my wedding. And I may have accidentally forgotten to tell my mom.

And by "accidentally" I mean, I *purposely* did not tell my mom.

You see, my mom loves me but she REALLY LOVED my hair.

Now before you assume my mom is one of those shallow women who is all about appearances and whose daughter ultimately ends up miserable because of her overbearing mother – that is NOT our story. My mother is loving and kind but part of the reason she's that way is because her mother... wasn't, at least not with her.

See mom was from one of THOSE families. Her mother was a debutante. Both of her grandfathers were doctors, graduates of Meharry Medical School, and everyone in her family could pass the infamous paper bag test, as in they were all lighter than a paper bag. Mom was one of four girls, one more gorgeous than the next. Truth be told, I always considered mom to be more beautiful than her sisters, but of course I'm biased.

But in her family mom was not considered beautiful for one reason: her hair. Her sisters had "good hair" as they used to say, with curls down to their waists. But mom had kinky hair that barely grew past her ear. It was honey colored, almost blonde. Her mother used to say, "At least she has that going for her." But that let my mother know that in *her* mother's eyes, she was less than. But mom married my father, a doctor, and then she had me. And I DIDN'T have her hair. I had "good hair."

As I grew up it became hard to reconcile the woman who flew down to spoil me for all of my birthdays, with the woman whose coldness caused my mother to tremble in her presence.

When I was in elementary school Andy Dobson was playing with scissors and cut his hair and mine. I found it hysterical. I was a kid. What did I know? But mom was a different kind of hysterical. That was the first time I saw her cry. I didn't understand. But I found out years later she actually told my grandmother I was sick so she wouldn't visit for my birthday that year. Mom was waiting for my hair to grow back.

To my father's amusement and my mother's horror I'd always been pretty adventurous. I loved rock climbing, skydiving... in fact that's how I met my fiancé. We actually planned to spend our entire honeymoon diving... in some of the world's most beautiful bodies of water. But my long, curly hair got in the way during my scuba lessons. So I decided to chop it all off.

I LOVED the way it looked. My fiancé did too. He said I transformed from beautiful to smoking hot.

I knew I'd never go back to wearing it long again. But as my mother cried, I didn't tell her that. Instead I just walked over to her in my wedding gown and said: "Mom. It's okay. I know I will never be as beautiful as you, even on my wedding day. But, I cut my hair so I could look a little more like you because I've always considered you the most beautiful woman in the world."

She took my face in her hands, closed her eyes and leaned her head on my shoulder. She then whispered, "You look beautiful, and I love you."

6. Little Blessing

(The piece below is ideally delivered as previously recorded audio, with either images of a Black mother on screen or images of Black motherhood conveyed in some other way.)

AUDIO. She was so tiny and so beautiful and I loved her sooo much. We had tried for a really long time. But I gotta be honest. I didn't complain about the morning sickness, which was pretty bad. I didn't complain about the weight gain, which was a lot. I thought I was a pretty good sport about all of that. But the post-partum hair loss, they call it, well I know it sounds crazy to say this, but that was tougher on me than giving birth. Again, I know that sounds crazy. I was so happy to have my beautiful baby girl. But I was so sad to lose part of myself, to literally see pieces of me disappear down the drain every day. I would just sit there in the shower and cry. I didn't tell anyone. I was too embarrassed. Then my sorority sister, Monique, almost died in childbirth and her baby was stillborn. I had no idea so many Black women still die giving birth, even today, until that happened. That night as I was rocking Imani to sleep in my arms and she put her little hand on my scalp, well... it was the best feeling in the world. She's my little princess.

(To **IMANI.***)* "Yes you are. Mommy's little princess. And I love you so much."

7. Adaora and Her Little Princess

(This monologue is ideally delivered in an African accent. [A working class British accent could possibly be substituted depending on the production.])

What a day to celebrate. Who would believe it? A girl from Africa from humble roots.

And here I was at... A ROYAL WEDDING!

(Pause. She smiles and straightens her back with pride. She then pulls out a pair of binoculars then says...)

My sister said that standing outside St. George's Chapel in a crowd of strangers was not the same as truly attending the royal wedding.

I told my sister that her negative attitude was why she could never find a husband.

My daughter and I had arrived early, the day before and slept outside to make sure we would have an ideal view of Prince Harry and the American Meghan Markle when they waved to the crowd *(She waves.)* following their royal wedding. And my daughter would one day be able to say she was part of history.

(She pulls out a tiara and heavily feathered fascinator hat and a poster that reads, "ENGLAND LOVES OUR AMERICAN PRINCESS MEGHAN".)

Some people may think it's silly to celebrate a wedding for someone you do not know. And by some people I mean my sister said, "It is silly to celebrate a wedding for someone you do not know." She then brought up the fact that I did not attend the wedding of my own cousin

Adankwo. But as I told her, that is not a comparable scenario or circumstance... because I do not like my cousin.

My sister then said, "How can you say you like Meghan Markle or Prince Harry? You do not even know them."

And I said, "Well maybe if I did not know our cousin, I would still like her. But I DO know her, and I do not."

One of my friends does not care for the royal family. She does not care for royalty at all. She says they smile and wave in pretty dresses that cost more than we earn in a year and we should protest them, not celebrate them.

I'm not very political and never have been. But for me the royal wedding of Prince Harry and Meghan Markle is not about politics.

It's about my daughter. You see her father is no longer with us.

(Pause.)

Oh, he's not dead. But if my papa ever sees him again he might kill him.

You see my daughter's father was – is – handsome, and charming. He called himself a mutt: part French, Irish, Russian, and Czech. In America they just called him white.

As in my aunt who lived there said, "Where you meet that white boy?"

I met him at school. I was not one of those silly girls who has a baby with a boy just because he tells her she is pretty.

He told me I was pretty AND smart.

And then came the baby.

He came around the first month of her life, my daughter's papa. Then he just went away. He had family in America. I heard he was there.

And I was left here with a baby.

A baby who looked nothing like me.

In the posh neighborhoods ladies always thought I was the nanny. When she was five she was naughty and as I was dragging her home a woman said, *(Imitating an upper class British accent.)* "If you don't release that child at once I will call Scotland Yard."

And I turned around and said, "Call them. So I can tell them some crazy lady is disturbing me and my daughter."

She was shocked so I asked her if she would like to see my birthing scar.

She declined.

It has been said that in England we do not have the problems with race that America does. I once heard someone say "No one cares what color you are in the United Kingdom…

…we just care what class you are."

He said that like it was a good thing. But I'm not sure that it is.

I am also not sure if it is true. I have never been to America.

But I do know that my little one used to be happy until she started at her new school. She does not look like the other girls there.

She has light brown skin and freckles and long light brown hair with large round curls, except for at the very top of her head. The hair at the very top of her head is pure African hair. I broke a comb on that one piece of hair when she was small. When she saw her cousins got braids she begged me for braids too. I tried to tell her that her hair was not like theirs but she would not hear it. When I finished with her braids she did not look like her cousins at all but like a little tan Bo Derek. And then the girls at school teased her and so she cried some more.

She asked me if she was ugly. Which was very silly. She is the most beautiful little girl.

I know all mothers say this but in the case of my little girl it is true. *(She smiles.)*

I tried to show her photographs of Barack Obama so she could see someone like her, someone who has one parent who is African and one parent who is something else, can be a success.

She asked me if I was saying she looked like an old man.

So when Prince Harry announced his engagement to the American Meghan Markle and they showed a photograph of her with her mother, I showed my little girl. I said, you see, this is who we are like.

Her eyes grew very wide. She just stared and stared and then asked:

"Can we go see her?"

And so here we are. At the royal wedding so that my little princess can see a real life princess who looks like her.

> *(She pauses. Smiles grabs her poster and motions down as if to her daughter.)*

Here they come!!!!

>   *(She waves her hand then holds up her poster.)*

She waved back at us!!! She waved!

The princess waved at my little princess!!!

8. Tracy and the Trip

*(A lady appears on the stage wearing braids.
She is full of hope and optimism.)*

TRACY. When he saw me at the airport he told me I looked like a Nubian princess.

See I had met T.J. at church... *(Pause.)*

Well we told everyone we met at church.

We actually met on a dating app, which I know is perfectly normal now, but not to my mom who is convinced going on a date with a stranger you met on the internet is like applying to be the subject of a *Dateline* episode where a woman goes missing.

And I know telling a lie about church is... well, kind of tacky... but in my defense, we do both go to the same church now and frankly I feel like if you're a woman dating online, then I just assume that God forgives you in advance for all of the dating related lies you'll probably tell.

(She then does a different voice to denote she's quoting things she's said in online dating profiles.)

"What a coincidence! I LOVE mixed martial arts AND video games too! Sure, I'd love to meet up!"

"Swimming with sharks? Of course that's on my bucket list! Isn't it on everybody's?"

But T.J. was the first guy in a long time I didn't feel the need to lie to. You know?

We were going away on our very first trip... to Mexico. And everyone – and I DO MEAN EVERYONE, said that your first major trip is often make or break for couples. So I wanted it to be perfect...

The only thing is T.J. had never seen me without my weave. Now I wasn't one of those women who thought I was ugly without a weave, but I was wearing one in the photo on my dating profile and there was never a perfect moment to mention that that's not how my hair always looked. So I figured I'd ease into things on our trip.

I did what I always do when I leave the country: I got braids so I wouldn't have to worry about my hair. T.J. loved *Poetic Justice* and said when he was a kid he had a big crush on Janet Jackson after seeing the movie. But when the stylist finished my braids... well I kind of didn't look like Janet Jackson... at all...

> *(We see the disappointment on her face and we hear the* **VOICE** *from the audio that opened the show say...)*

A VOICE OFFSTAGE.   "Honey. I'm a hairstylist not a magician. I can give you Janet Jackson's hair but I can't make you look like her. NO ONE CAN."

> *(We see disappointment turn to irritation.)*

TRACY.   I made a mental note never to go back to her again. Half my scalp needed CBD oil because some of her braids were so tight. The other half didn't seem quite tight enough but T.J. said he liked my braids and once we kicked off our vacay I was too busy having an AMAZING time with him to really think about my hair. That's how I knew I was falling in love. We became one of those couples I used to make fun of. You know, holding hands as we strolled on the beach. He even got me into the water. I usually hate the water. But I was so happy I didn't even think about it when we fell into the tide and my braids got wet.

The synthetic hair used in my braids took FOREVER to dry so for hours it looked like someone was peeing down my shoulder. But nothing was going to ruin my mood or our trip... At least that's what I thought.

It was our last night together. The trip had been PERFECT.

If this was a test of our relationship, we'd passed with flying colors. We were sitting at an outdoor restaurant by the water, watching the sun go down, gazing into each other's eyes over the best margaritas I've ever tasted, like we were in a scene from a black Hallmark movie, when a waiter appeared and said:

"Senora, I do believe this is yours."

I looked down and there I saw it. One of my jumbo box braids had fallen off of my head and landed on his drinks tray.

(Pause.)

So of course I said, what any self-respecting woman in my shoes would have:

"No señor. I believe you must have me confused with someone else."

Looking back I now realize that might not have been the most strategic defense, considering we were the ONLY Black couple in the restaurant and I was the ONLY person wearing braids. But what else was I gonna say????

When he persisted, I then said the only thing I could think of:

"No habla Ingles..." which again, I now realize may not have been the wisest way to go... you know... because the waiter spoke Spanish... and I don't... but again... hindsight's 20/20.

The poor waiter looked utterly confused. I couldn't look him or T.J. in the eye. All three of us just sat in an awkward silence until T.J. finally said:

"You heard the lady. She said it's not hers. Please find the person it belongs to."

(Pause.)

That was the moment I knew I'd marry him. Because no matter how crazy I sounded, this man clearly had my back. And isn't that ultimately what we're all looking for?

On the way out of the restaurant I saw him slip the waiter a twenty and then T.J. told me I looked more beautiful than Janet Jackson in *Poetic Justice*.

9. Wanda and the Campaign

(A **LADY** *stands on the stage. She exudes warmth AND strength.)*

WANDA. When he told me I was beautiful and that my HAIR was BEAUTIFUL ...

That was it. Love at first sight.

See my brothers had teased me about my "nappy" hair as far back as I can remember. In their defense I do have "nappy hair." But the difference is I grew up thinking that was a bad thing and it was only once I got to college that I embraced my natural hair in all its nappy glory. But there were still plenty of guys like my brothers, who were...not happy with nappy...

Which is why when Askari walked over to me and said, "I love your hair. It's beautiful." That was it for me. But it wasn't just that he loved my hair. He loved James Baldwin and conscious rappers like Common. He said, despite the artistry he simply couldn't support work by talented rappers who didn't lift up Black women as the Queens that we are, in their lyrics. He told me India Arie was the most underappreciated artist of our lifetime, a modern day Nina Simone.

And then he said he was looking for his Winnie – as in the Winnie to his Nelson... as in Mandela. And he said he knew he'd found her when he met me. And that's when he told me he was running for President...

(Pause for dramatic effect...)

...of the Black Graduate Students Association. Even though technically there was no official First Lady role, Askari told me I would be HIS first lady and this would be the first campaign of many.

The only real competition was Deshaun Sanders who had been a standout athlete before an injury took him out of the running – no pun intended – for his shot at the NFL. He was popular and charming, in that way good-looking athletes are, which drove Askari insane. During one campaign event, Askari made a point to say that in addition to the issues he wanted to advocate on as President, the other reason to vote for him is he didn't just talk the talk on civil rights and racial justice, he walked the walk in his personal life and that supporting him meant getting a two for one deal because his girlfriend, me, a Black woman, would help him effectively advocate on issues that mattered to Black women on campus.

I saw Deshaun flinch when Askari said it. See Deshaun's girlfriend was white. So Askari was basically saying: "How can you advocate for us publicly when privately you won't choose one of your own?" I mean I didn't actually feel this way, but I knew there were other people who did. But frankly I thought it was kind of ironic Askari was even raising the issue because... well Askari's mom is white.

Askari actually looked a lot like his mom. In fact he sort of resembled Drake, but with dreads.

   (Pause for that to sink in...)

Anyway, we all know that one debate performance can make or break a campaign, so I knew I had to be by his side during his first townhall face-off with Deshaun. I had an interview for an internship that day, but I raced back to campus to be with my baby. But when I went up to give him a good luck kiss he looked... embarrassed.

All he said was, "What did you do to your hair?"

See I had gotten it pressed straight for my interview because I was told the hiring manager was pretty conservative.

Askari looked at me with disgust and said, "You should go."

So I left, and later that night we had our first and last argument. He told me that part of what drew him to me was that he wanted a woman who was as committed to embracing her authentic Black identity as he was committed to embracing his. And that by straightening my hair I was pulling a bait and switch on him, and in the middle of a close campaign.

(She takes a moment to let the offensiveness sink in...)

So I told him, first of all "Slow your roll, Barack," you're not running for the Democratic nomination, you're running for President of an association with like fifty members, tops. I also told him if he was serious about embracing his "authentic Black identity" *(She does bunny gestures to denote "quote".)* he might want to start with his own name which was Grant Pierre Witherspoon III, not Askari which is Swahili for warrior. I also told him that considering he was half white it was a little ridiculous that he was always policing other people's blackness like he was a direct descendant of Shaka Zulu or something.

He then told me that Winnie never would have talked to Nelson Mandela that way.

And I told him Nelson Mandela and Barack Obama both became Presidents – REAL Presidents – because they were smart enough to choose women who were strong enough NOT to let a man tell them how to wear their hair.

He told me supporting my journey as a naturalista was not the same as pressuring me to adhere to European standards of beauty.

I told him it's MY hair. My body. My choice. And whether I want to wear my hair natural or wear it pressed OR relaxed, I don't need a man telling me what to do. It's a form of patriarchal control and I told him I wasn't having it.

He then told me if that's how I felt, I could go back to being single...

(Pause.)

...just like lots of other Black women.

(We see the hurt on her face.)

He stormed out and that was that.

Or so he thought.

I did what I do after a breakup. I listened to some Mary J. Blige. I watched *Waiting to Exhale*. And then the next day I went to the salon. Only unlike Ms. Angela Bassett's Bernadine in *Waiting to Exhale*, I DIDN'T go to get my hair cut off after my man did me wrong.

A few days later I strutted into the next townhall debate wearing a blonde weave that went all the way down to my butt and I made sure to ask Grant Pierre – and yes that's what I called him – and DeShaun if they felt women who choose to relax their hair or wear hair extensions are less authentically Black than women who do not. There were audible gasps from the sisters in that room. DeShaun replied, "Of course not. First off, it's not my place or any man's place, to tell any sister how she should wear her hair." The room burst into applause, everyone except Askari that is. I then noticed that the sisters in the room began glancing back and forth between Askari and me. *(She glances back and forth like watching a tennis match.)* Askari and me. Askari and me.

I didn't have to say another word.

But get this, later that evening another brother said, "You know I really love your hair. The blonde really suits you."

I thanked him. But I had realized something. When it comes to my hair, the only opinion that really matters, is my own.

(She exits – victorious.)

10. It's Just Hair

*(We see the **LADY** who portrayed the **ACTRESS** in the play's opening scene take the stage. She stares before a mirror. She takes a seat. The chair can either be made to look as if it is located in a hair salon, or simply in her own bathroom where she has products around her denoting she is about to attempt a chemical relaxer.)*

(We hear...)

VOICE OF THE CASTING DIRECTOR OFF STAGE. *(Echoing their earlier exchange from the audition.)* You're just so talented. I'd hate for something as silly as how you CHOOSE to wear your hair to hurt your chances.

I mean this show could change your whole life. And after all, it's just hair.

(The lady continues to stare at herself in the mirror and says...)

ACTRESS. It's just hair. I can change it. It's not a big deal. It's just hair.

(At this point instrumental music begins to play* – whether an African drum, a saxophone, or even the sounds of a tambourine or clapping, the music is up to the director and whatever is best suited to the venue. But throughout the poem's delivery, imagery representing the historical moments being referenced should appear on stage in

---

* A license to produce THE GLORIOUS WORLD OF CROWNS, KINKS AND CURLS does not include a performance license for any third-party or copyrighted music. Licensees should create an original composition or use music in the public domain. For further information, please see Music Use Note on page 3.

some capacity, whether via film, or posters or
silhouettes or slides.*)

It's not who I am. It's just hair.

(And then the voices of the other two actresses
can either be heard reciting the poem that
follows, or they can actually be seen on stage
with the **ACTRESS** *– only she should not act*
as though she is aware of their presence at
all. Starting with her reflection in the mirror,
she eventually begins what is essentially a
dialogue/debate with herself. The delivery
of the poem should increase in speed, until
reaching its crescendo at the end.)

LADY 1. For some, Black beauty and Black women's hair
has always been dangerous.

So it's been debated, regulated, turned into a source of
anguish.

ACTRESS. It's just hair.

LADY 2. In 1786 Governor Esteban Miro introduced the
Tiyon Law.

He deemed the beauty of women of color too alluring
and too raw.

So they were made to wear head scarves so they could
be easily identified.

But if you want to make Black women LESS attractive
don't give them something fabulous to accessorize.

LADY 1. Scarves or no scarves, their beauty was undeniable.

And yet throughout history the impact of racist beauty standards has been sadly, reliable.

ACTRESS. It's just hair.

LADY 2. During slavery, having straight hair might mean your Master was also your father,

So you might not work in the fields, but you were still seen as a slave not his son or daughter.

LADY 1. But as Maya Angelou reminded us, we always rise and have always endured.

And at the start of the 20th century Black women came into their power as beauty entrepreneurs.

LADY 2. Though a Black man, Garrett Morgan created the hair relaxer and the stoplight,

It was Black women for whom the business of hair would truly take flight.

LADY 1. After losing her own hair to products that left her mamed,

Madam C.J. Walker made sure we'd never forget her name.

She went around selling hair products door to door,

But for the Black women she served there was much more in store.

She wasn't just selling products or potions or creams.

She was empowering Black women who'd long felt invisible, to feel seen.

ACTRESS. It's just hair.

LADY 2. Walker would use her success in beauty to fight the ugliness of lynching.

Because no matter how far you soar, the realities of racism are heart-wrenching.

She learned her trade from Annie Turnbo Malone,

Who many have forgotten but whose name should also be known.

Malone was one of the first Black hair beauty queens.

She inspired Madam C.J. Walker and other women to dream.

ACTRESS. It's just hair.

LADY 1. During the Civil Rights era the glamour of Diana Ross and Coretta Scott King reigned Supreme,

Their fashions and hairstyles became iconic, and entered the mainstream.

But by the late 1960's beauty standards were changing when it came to hair.

Soon, there were chants of "BLACK POWER" in the air.

LADY 2. Afros weren't just a symbol of Black power and Black beauty,

For some, how you chose to wear your hair became about duty.

ACTRESS. It's just hair.

LADY 1. In the 1970s news anchor Jocelyn Dorsey rocked an afro on air without fear.

The move took courage, because even today going natural can, sadly, hurt your career.

ACTRESS. It's just hair.

LADY 2. In the 1980s and 90s America finally got Black beauty queens.

All diverse in their beauty, except for their hair it seems.

There was a beauty queen standard pageants still had.

It wasn't that complicated: straight good. Kinky bad.

ACTRESS. It's just hair.

LADY 1. But in 2019 history was made.

All the major beauty queens were Black, and came in every shade.

They represented the spectrum of Black beauty and Black hair.

Long, short, kinky, curly, but ALL glorious, in case you weren't aware.

LADY 2. Because of these queens other women and girls will know that they are queens too.

Regardless of how many times someone tries to demean you.

ACTRESS. It's just hair!

LADY 1. Chris Rock and Spike Lee have both been talkin' 'bout good and bad hair,

If you've got curly 3A texture, you're good, but if you've got kinky 4C, the world will despair.

ACTRESS. It's just hair!

LADY 2. From America, to Europe, Africa and around the world.

The struggle for self-love and hair love, is universal, especially for our girls.

ACTRESS. It's just hair!

LADY 1. But as more politicians pass laws to protect our natural CROWNS,

The future looks brighter for all of us, not just in big cities, but in every small town.

ACTRESS. It's just hair!

LADY 2. Fewer boys will be forced to cut their dreads on a wrestling mat,

Fewer girls will be shamed for their afros, locks, twists and plaits.

ACTRESS. It's just hair!!!!

LADY 1. Black hair IS Black power.

LADY 2. It's Black beauty.

ACTRESS. It's Black pain.

LADY 1. It's also Black joy, and knowing your hair looks just fine even if it gets wet in the rain.

ACTRESS. It takes time to undo years of history telling us we don't belong.

LADY 1. But it starts with the girls in my life –

LADY 2. And YOUR life –

ACTRESS. So I hope you will teach them this poem, this song.

ACTRESS, LADY 1 & LADY 2. Because if girls know about ALL of the Black women who came before them who want them to feel like queens,

(The music stops.)

ACTRESS. Then maybe one day we can stop writing plays about hair and stop passing laws, because we will FINALLY live in a world where all Black girls feel loved, beautiful and seen.

(Lights out. They exit.)

11. Rhonda and Red Lobster

(**RHONDA** *stands on the stage, her aura conveying kindness and justice.*)

RHONDA. For as long as I can remember I always wanted to grow up and have the kind of career where I could make a difference in the world. And I was finally on the brink of realizing that dream. So to celebrate the biggest day of my life my fiancé made us a reservation at...

RED LOBSTER.

Now I know that may not sound so fancy to some, but as broke as we were it might as well have been the fanciest restaurant in the world. The two of us had over three hundred thousand dollars, combined, in student loan debt. But it was all worth it because Jamal had just landed a residency at his dream hospital and tonight I would find out if I had landed the Thurgood Marshall Civil Rights fellowship at my dream law firm.

I wasn't just waiting to hear from any law firm... but a law firm that counted four United States Senators and two Supreme Court Justices as former lawyers there. My dream had been to become the first Black woman on the Supreme Court and my family and Jamal had cheered me on every step along the way. Jamal and I met in the library on a Saturday night. He asked to borrow my highlighter and well... that was that.

He always dreamed of becoming a doctor so he could help people like his mom who had a chronic illness. And I had always dreamed of becoming a lawyer after learning that the Brown versus the Board of Education decision was the reason I got to attend my school.

The year my sister dressed up as Wonder Woman for Halloween, I dressed up as Constance Baker Motley: the first Black female federal judge, the first Black woman to argue a case before the Supreme Court, and she also helped Thurgood Marshall litigate and win Brown versus the Board of Education.

My mother called my costume clever and original. The other kids called it... weird.

But today all of my nerdy weirdness was going to pay off.

Now here we were on the cusp of realizing our American Dream.

I didn't technically know for sure I'd landed the fellowship. But I knew the interview had gone great – better than great. I could see it in their eyes: they liked me and in career coaching they tell you a lot of hiring decisions come down to that. Would someone want to make small talk with you in an airport if your flight got cancelled? We were all having so much fun chatting that my interview actually ran twenty minutes over.

And I had an ally. My mentor, who was now retired but had been the first black female partner at the firm, told me she put in a good word for me and that it was looking good.

So, Jamal made us a reservation at Red Lobster for eight p.m.

At five p.m. I got the call from my mentor letting me know the firm had, quote, "decided to go in a different direction."

At first I was speechless. But eventually I managed to tell her that I was grateful for all of her help and that I would be sure to send thank you notes to them, for considering me. I was hoping she wouldn't be able to tell that I was on the verge of tears. But before hanging up, I couldn't resist asking if there was anything I could've done differently. She told me they all really liked me and that it had been close. Then she hesitated before asking if I had changed my hair.

It took me a minute to register the question. My hair? And then she asked if I still wore it down.

I explained that most of the time I wear it down, but I know the firm is kinda old-school conservative so I pulled it back in a bun for my interviews.

See I had always had the kind of hair that was half curly and half kinky. So I didn't even bother trying to tame it most of the time. It was a lost cause. I just wore it loose and natural. Occasionally I'd put a headband on. Except for special occasions when I'd pull it back, and interviewing for the job of my dreams, seemed like a special occasion, so...

I could hear my mentor sigh. She then told me that if I really wanted to hear the truth, the truth is the partners who made the decision couldn't tell that I was Black.

(She lets this sink in.)

The firm had faced criticism for their lack of diversity since her retirement and since this position was a high profile Civil Rights fellowship...

I couldn't believe it. She told me to keep my chin up and we said our goodbyes... and then I began to cry, really cry... ugly cry.

I mean we have to worry about our hair being seen as unprofessional if it looks too natural or too wild. But now I have to worry about someone not believing I'm Black enough if I don't wear my hair the way they expect me to. It's exhausting, not just dealing with our hair, but the mental energy we have to waste thinking about it all the time.

I looked in the mirror. Despite my light eyes and light curls I still see a Black woman staring back at me. I've never seen anything else. But I know what other people sometimes see. I know some people see immense privilege, someone who "thinks she's cute." For the record I spent high school with acne and braces, so I haven't spent too much of my life thinking I'm cute.

But I also know that I have always had a much easier time hailing a cab than my mom and my sisters, all of whom are darker than me.

So while losing that job hurt, I decided not to dwell on the moment where having light eyes and light hair may not have helped.

Instead, I called up my mom and my sisters and said: "Hey, I miss you guys. Wanna join me and Jamal at Red Lobster tonight?"

12. Office Politics

(**ALLY** *comes rushing into an office with a piece of rolling luggage. She is a young lawyer – full of optimism. The other woman,* **SHARON** *is an older partner at the firm where they work. When the scene begins* **SHARON** *is busy looking down at a folder and doesn't see Ally at first but is listening to her.*)

ALLY. I'm here! I'm here! Johnny wasn't exactly thrilled that he will now be dining at our favorite restaurant... out of state, by himself, on our anniversary tonight. But I told him I would join as soon as I can and as you always remind me, you have to make sacrifices early in your career to enjoy the fruits of your labor later.

SHARON. That's right...

(*She looks up.*)

What did you do to your hair?

ALLY. Oh I always get it cornrowed when I go on vacation. I was supposed to be away this week... for my anniversary trip... that I'm now missing...

SHARON. Ally, our client is from an old Boston Brahmin family.

ALLY. Okay...

SHARON. The only Black people he regularly interacts with are his maids.

ALLY. Okay...

SHARON. No. This is NOT okay. I lobbied the other partners to get you on this case.

ALLY. And I appreciate it which is why I left my husband – who used up all of his remaining vacation days at work to take me on this trip – at the airport by himself so I could come here on a Saturday to work on this case.

SHARON. I'm sorry. I can't let you meet a major client looking like this.

ALLY. The guy is accused of embezzling millions of dollars. I think he has bigger fish to fry than worrying about how I wear my hair.

SHARON. You ungrateful brat.

(**ALLY** *is stunned and caught completely off guard.*)

ALLY. I beg your pardon...

SHARON. When I started here in 1989 you know where they put me?

At a receptionist's desk. The first year I was here every client, or process server or pizza delivery guy, assumed I was a secretary. It wasn't because they didn't have office space. It was to humiliate me, to break me. But I wouldn't let it.

They would exclude me from meetings. The meetings they did bother to include me in they wouldn't acknowledge me – even when I spoke – they acted like I was invisible except for one partner who would ask me what I thought of last night's episode of *The Cosby Show* every week. It was his favorite show but that's not why he was asking. He was asking to embarrass me. To make me extra conscious of my blackness and the fact that I didn't belong. Sometimes he'd even call me Claire Huxtable but I just laughed and kept my head down and did the work. And fifteen years later, I'm still here and he's not.

And I'm a partner. And I decided when I finally had the power I was going to use it to make the journey for the next Black woman that came behind me easier. I wasn't going to be one of those women who pulled up the ladder behind me once I reached the top. I was going to help a sister up the ladder even if it meant hearing them whisper behind my back, "You see. I knew the first thing she'd do is start filling the firm with *them* if we gave her the chance."

And now you're standing here with an attitude because I'm telling you the truth which is that your hair will make it that much harder for me to convince them to let another sister climb up behind you.

ALLY. It's just hair, Sharon.

SHARON. God, I wish that were true.

>   *(Pause.)*

But if you really believe that, then you should go back to the airport and join your husband.

ALLY. Are you kidding?

>   (**SHARON** *turns around and goes back to work.*)

SHARON. No, I'm not.

>   (**ALLY** *is pissed and hurt and turns to go.*)

ALLY. I do appreciate everything you've done for me. I'm sorry that this... that I... my hair will be back to normal when I get back...

SHARON. Ally, my advice is that you should spend your vacation looking for another job.

ALLY. Wait a minute... you're firing me?

SHARON. No. But you've shown me today that you don't have what it takes to last here. And I don't want waste the political capital I've accumulated over the last fiftteen years on the wrong person.

Look it's 2004. Maybe one day we'll live in a world where cornrows in a courtroom will be just as common on judges as they are on defendants. But until then, you may want to find something else to do that's more befitting your attitude and personality.

(**ALLY** *stands there with a mixture of hurt and anger. Then we see it morph into empathy.*)

ALLY. Sharon, I really admire you and am grateful for every door that you've opened.

SHARON. Thank you for saying that.

ALLY. But I am so sorry this place has wounded you and your spirit in the way it clearly has. And I hope one day if I ever make it as far as you have, that the conversation the 2014 or 2020 version of me has with a younger lawyer is different.

(She exits.)

13. Chantal's Fierce Magic

*(The costumes and décor should denote that
the* **LADY** *in this scene is strong, proud and
working class.)*

CHANTAL. Mama once told me you could never trust
lawyers. They think they're better than other people.
And after I finally met one I knew why she felt that
way.

Shakeem was the only person I would trust to do my
hair when it mattered and it REALLY mattered now
after what that lawyer said. Shakeem and I had known
each other since we were kids. I was the first person he
ever told he was gay. He even moved in with mama and
me after his parents kicked him out when he told them.
He and I would watch *Mahogany* over and over again.
It was our favorite movie. So that's one of the reasons
I brought him a photo of Diana Ross from *Mahogany*.
I knew he'd love it. I knew he'd love trying to make me
look like her. And I knew it would help us both relax,
cause deep down we were both nervous.

One of the people from the DA's office had asked me if
I needed help gettin' ready. I told her I felt as ready as I
was gonna be. We been over my testimony... a lot.

I almost felt like a actress learnin' lines, but they kept
tellin' me they didn't want me to sound rehearsed.
"Juries can be suspicious of what you're sayin' if you
sound too polished, too rehearsed," they'd told me.

Then why'd they keep rehearsin' with me, I wanted to
know.

But then the lawyer lady told me that's not what she
meant. She asked if I needed help with my hair and
makeup for that day.

It was weird. They didn't want me to sound like an actress in court, but here they were offerin' to help me get ready like a movie star going to the Oscars.

I mean who doesn't want a makeover? It sounded like it could be... well, fun's not the right word, but like a nice distraction from it all.

Then she finally said what she meant though she had trouble lookin' me in the eye when she said it. First she said she believed me. That they all did. That's why they were fightin' so hard to help me, and the other women get justice.

But she told me that juries don't just make decisions based on what you say, but how you present yourself... how you look.

And she told me that she was worried that when jurors looked at me, they might not see a victim.

(She begins to cry.)

They might see my long sparkly nails, and the tattoo on my neck and my blue and pink braids, and my makeup, and decide I don't remind them of their wives or daughters.

I asked her what my hair and makeup had to do with that animal slippin' something in my drink and doin' God knows what to me.

And I do mean only God knows... God and him. I don't remember anything. Just wakin' up on the floor in my kitchen with nothin' on. And I thought because I didn't remember, that it was my fault, until two other girls at the store said he did it to them.

He said the same thing to all of us. That he worried about us takin' the subway late at night by ourselves and as our manager he felt it was his duty to take care of us. So he gave us all rides home.

Anyway, I told Shakeem when it happened. I knew if I told mama she'd blame me. I'd heard her talk about girls who she said got themselves into trouble by being alone with a man. "What'd they think was gonna happen?" She would say.

Shakeem told me to go to the police. But I told him what mama had always said and that he was a manager of a big store. I was just a cashier.

But when I found out he'd done it to other girls I wanted to help.

So here I am, trying to help and the attorney who's supposed to be on our side is here tellin' me that people might not believe me because of the way I wear my hair.

She said I should wear a black or gray suit and "minimal makeup" and pull my hair back into a "tasteful" bun or ponytail. She said "tasteful" REAL slow... like she was worried I didn't know the meaning of the word.

I probably should have thanked her. After all she's only trying to help us... but instead I told her where she could go. Then I went home... and cried... and cried.

When I finished, I went out and bought a cheap gray suit. It was ugly and it itched. I certainly felt like a fashion victim in it... *(Pause.)* So maybe the jury would see me as a victim after all.

But then I called Shakeem and made an appointment.

I may have been itchy and I may have been in an ugly suit, but my hair looked FIERCE. And this may sound silly but it made me FEEL FIERCE. And when I walked into that courtroom, I held my head high. I stared him down and told the truth about what he did and how it made me feel... afraid and ashamed.

But I wasn't ashamed anymore.

(She exits.)

14. The Beauty of Representation

(Like the earlier scene titled, "Little Blessing," the piece below should ideally be delivered as either previously recorded audio, or with one of the **LADIES** *voicing it from offstage, with imagery used to tell the story of the evolution of black female journalists.*)*

AUDIO. I had always cared deeply about representation, about making sure that Black girls got to see someone who looked like them on the news, since I rarely did growing up. I had planned to become the Black Barbara Walters but my hair was always an issue – not for me but for my bosses. My well-meaning, but often white, often male, often bald, bosses. My hair was never straight enough or long enough and I was getting sick and tired of dealing with it and then I actually got sick – for real. Really sick. I got cancer, my hair fell out during treatment and I started reevaluating what's important. I didn't want a life where what was on my head dictated my success so much. So I switched gears and picked a path that allowed me to focus on the ideas *in* my head instead. I became a professor, a journalism professor, and I have no regrets. Watching these younger Black women journalists wear their hair on television however they damn well please... well that gives me just as much joy as I ever could have gotten by becoming the Black Barbara Walters. Because I know these amazing women are making a difference just by changing the image of what a journalist looks like for the girls who are growing up watching them today.

---

* A license to produce THE GLORIOUS WORLD OF CROWNS, KINKS AND CURLS does not include a license to publicly display any third-party or copyrighted images. Licensees must acquire rights for any copyrighted images or create their own.

(Images of Black female journalists who wear their hair in nontraditional styles appear on stage: such as Athena Jones of CNN, Michel Martin of NPR, Farai Chideya, AJ Walker of News 12, Briana Collins of FOX Illinois, Orlando anchor Jazmin Bailey, Yamiche Alcindor of PBS and Samaria Terry.*)

---

* A license to produce THE GLORIOUS WORLD OF CROWNS, KINKS AND CURLS does not include a license to publicly display any third-party or copyrighted images. Licensees must acquire rights for any copyrighted images or create their own.

15. You Have Beautiful Hair

*(The **REPORTER** speaks with an American accent. The **REFUGEE** speaks with an African accent that can be altered depending on the audience. They should be on different parts of the stage and not interact until the scene's conclusion.)*

REPORTER. The irony of course is that I never cared what my hair looked like.

REFUGEE. Hair is very important to what you look like.

REPORTER. I mean I cared about Black women and girls having the chance to see someone who looks like them tell stories that matter to them. But when you don't know the next time you're going to get to shower or whether or not you're going to wake up in the morning, hair is the last thing on your mind.

REFUGEE. Mama did my braids.

REPORTER. My neighbor, Trina, would usually do my braids before I left on assignment. They were part of the Black female war reporter uniform. Would make sure I wouldn't have to worry about my hair while traveling abroad weeks, or months at a time.

REFUGEE. I used to love it when mama would do my braids. I had five brothers. She did everything for all of us. But when she did my braids – that time was just for us.

REPORTER. My mother used to tell me whenever I got braids that I looked like a teenager again.

REFUGEE. Mama would say my braids made me look like a woman.

(Both women put their hands to their hair, at the memory.)

REPORTER. Good reporters find ways to connect with any source, anywhere; find ways to break through language barriers, cultural barriers, to build trust. So I would often bond over the things that are universal, especially with other women. I once got a great interview just because a woman loved my braids.

　　　(Pause.)

I loved them too... until...

REFUGEE. I always loved the way my braids looked when mama finished.

REPORTER. No one talks about it. But every female reporter who goes on assignment, especially somewhere you know is dangerous, fears it. We all hear certain stories, like what happened to that CBS reporter in Egypt. But those are just the ones that become public. There are lots of them that don't. Mine didn't. I'd spent my career telling other people's stories, and yet when it happened to me I couldn't tell my own... I just couldn't talk about it... with anyone.

REFUGEE. In my culture you do not talk about such things. My husband was supposed to teach me what I needed to know when we were ready to have a baby.

REPORTER. This line of work isn't exactly great for relationships.

REFUGEE. I had not yet met my future husband.

REPORTER. When I told my fiancé I had to leave the country to cover an impending civil war on Christmas Eve, he said he'd had enough and told me I had to make a choice.

REFUGEE. Papa had not yet made his choice who he would allow to marry me.

REPORTER. What people don't understand is this is not just a job... it's a dream. It's a passion. Some might call it an obsession. My fiancé did. So if you force me to choose between you and this... you're going to be disappointed. My fiancé certainly was.

REFUGEE. An American volunteer in the camp asked me if I was disappointed my papa and brothers had a say in who I could marry. I asked her if finding a husband in America was much easier. She thought about it and then shook her head no.

REPORTER. The upside of being single again was I could take any assignment anywhere, without running it by anybody. That's why I didn't think twice about getting on a plane and just going. It wasn't even that dangerous of an assignment. *(Pause.)* At least it wasn't supposed to be.

REFUGEE. Of course we knew there was fighting. We had heard. My papa's sisters' two sons had come to stay with us after the rebels went through and destroyed their village.

But we thought... we thought...

REPORTER. It hadn't even been declared a war zone. The State Department had flagged it for tourists, but any real trouble was supposed to be months and months away.

REFUGEE. My brothers said we would be fine. They could protect mama and me from any trouble. I believed them. Why would I not?

REPORTER. Obviously, I knew not to travel alone. If I wasn't with an American military unit, I always travelled with a male translator or guide or fixer... the guys news outlets hire on the ground to coordinate stuff in local communities. I wasn't a rookie.

REFUGEE. I would never travel to another village alone. We knew not to do such things.

REPORTER. I was experienced enough to know that if I had to go to the bathroom in the middle of a jungle or behind a building, to make sure my guide or translator was within earshot in case anyone tried anything. That you're prepared for.

REFUGEE. Mama was preparing a special meal. I walked to get more water from the well.

REPORTER. My translator started to walk with me. See, I'd travelled more than twelve hours and was exhausted and so close to where I needed to get to and then at this last checkpoint my bladder decides it can't hold it anymore. Of course there was no women's bathroom because no women worked there. So my translator insisted that they find somewhere appropriate for me to relieve myself. They finally said that the head official in charge of the checkpoint had a private bathroom I could use. My translator was walking with me and then they said that a guard would escort me. I would be taken care of, like a special honored guest.

REFUGEE. When I would walk I would sing. Singing always makes me happy. Or as the American volunteers say, "calms my nerves."

REPORTER. When I'm nervous I play with my hair. I don't even realize I'm doing it until someone else points it out. It was strange. I'd literally been in war zones with bombs dropping all around me and felt less afraid than I did walking down that hall. By the time we got to the bathroom, my nerves were... Well I had gotten my finger tangled in my braid I'd twisted it so much. I built my career on trusting my gut. I don't know why I didn't trust it that day. Why I went in there...

REFUGEE. I sometimes think I should not have walked there that day. Even though I had done it many, many days before.

REPORTER. The guard directed me into an office. The rest of the building was a total dump. And yet this private office and the bathroom in it looked like something out of Versailles. So I relaxed a little. I used the bathroom and then when I opened the door to leave...the guard was gone. But another man was there.

REFUGEE. I thought I heard voices. But I didn't see any villagers by the well. I continued walking. I got to the well... and then I saw him. The first soldier.

(They say these lines in unison.)

REPORTER. He told me I had beautiful hair.

REFUGEE. He told me I had beautiful hair.

(They stop speaking in unison.)

REPORTER. He reached for my braids and began touching them. He was smiling. Which actually made me much more scared.

REFUGEE. I was not scared – at first.

He reached for my braids and just kept saying how pretty they were. Then he said I was pretty too. And then I saw another soldier. And another.

And then I was scared.

REPORTER. When he stroked my cheek, I went from scared to terrified. But I tried not to show it. Then he said in English, that I was pretty, for an American woman. I swatted his hand away and told him not to touch me and then I said: "I am walking out that door. And you will let me. Or you will be in serious trouble..."

And then... and then he laughed.

That's when I knew I was in real trouble. And then he said, "Do you know how many reporters die in this country every day? Do you think anyone will care if something happens to you? If you just disappear?"

(Both women are on stage crying.)

REFUGEE. I did not want to return home after. I did not want to see my papa and my brothers. I was ashamed.

(Pause.)

And not just because they had... they had ensured I would not be able to find a proper husband. But... they had shaved my head after they finished... so everyone would know what they did. They marked me...

(She is sobbing.)

REPORTER. I didn't want to give him the satisfaction of knowing he had hurt me...not just physically but I didn't want him to believe that he robbed me of the dignity that I entered that room with. So I didn't cry and I kept my head up and stared him down as I walked out the door.

REFUGEE. I could not look at my papa. I could not look at anyone.

REPORTER. He actually looked annoyed. Annoyed that he hadn't destroyed me.

REFUGEE. My mama held me. She rocked me as I cried. She told me I was a good girl. She looked at me. She was the only one who would look at me, in my eyes.

REPORTER. I had been gone so long that when I got back downstairs my translator asked me if I was alright. I told him I was fine and that it was a really beautiful bathroom. And it was.

(She is crying.)

Later that night once we were settled in our tiny hotel, I cut my braids off. All of them. I looked like a mess, but I didn't care. I just wanted it all off my head.

REFUGEE. But because of what happened to me my village knew the fighting had come to all of us. I was told that what the soldiers did to me is a weapon of war.

REPORTER. Now I know why they call what he did to me a "weapon of war." Because the truth is I think getting shot and surviving would've hurt less. Maybe not physically, but definitely emotionally.

REFUGEE. I knew my father and brothers felt ashamed. None of them would look at me. They barely spoke to me, like I was bad. I asked mama if things would ever go back to the way they were. She told me things would never be the same again. Our country was descending into war. I asked her when things would be the same between papa and me. She told me when my hair grew back it would be easier for papa to look at me again... easier for everyone.

REPORTER. I never told anyone. Not my bosses at the network. Not my sister. I came close. The first time I saw her after that trip, she said I looked "different." I told her I'd changed my hair. She said that wasn't it. Something had shifted... in me. She could tell. So I almost told her. But then I thought of all those times she told me my job was too dangerous. That I was an attractive woman and an easy target...

I knew it wasn't my fault and I knew no one would ever say "I told you so," but there are so many people who believe this kind of work is too dangerous for women. I certainly wasn't going to let them think they're right. I had interviewed enough survivors to know that it does shift something. But the only tangible change I could see in my own life is that I never, ever wore braids again...

REFUGEE. Our lives did change. I lost two of my brothers to the war – conflict – they kept calling it. And one day, mama came back with her head shaved too.

REPORTER. I got diagnosed with post-traumatic stress disorder (PTSD) and made a deal with my doctor that I would slow down a bit. So I signed on to co-edit this book on *Women and War.* Instead of covering wars, I began interviewing all sorts of women who had been impacted by wars. Mothers who'd lost sons as soldiers, women who had been generals, a female warlord... and then I went to a refugee camp...

REFUGEE. It was my second year at a refugee camp. They told me a woman wanted to talk to me about war. The American aid worker who had become my friend told me not to be afraid. Not to be ashamed. That I could trust her. So I told her what the soldiers had done to me. That they told me I had beautiful hair and then they had hurt me.

> *(The two women turn and face each other and walk towards each other on stage.)*

It was strange. She grew very, very quiet. Then I could see that she was crying. I went to comfort her and she looked me in the eye and said...

> *(They say the next lines in unison.)*

Me too.

REPORTER. Me too.

> *(Lights down.)*

16. In Memoriam

(We see a middle-aged Black woman on the stage looking into a mirror. She is in a bathrobe and has rollers in her hair. She carefully begins removing the rollers, one by one.)

(On a different part of the stage, intended to represent a different room, we see a younger Black woman, her hair "wrapped," in the way many Black women wear their hair protectively to sleep without disturbing the smoothness of their hair through the night. She is wearing a house dress and also staring into a mirror. She begins taking the pins out of her hair one by one.)

(We watch each woman style her hair in silence. But at various moments, we see the women struggle with their emotions. Tears, anger... they may need to sit or lean to steady themselves.)

(They finish their hair at approximately the same time. When they are finished, each woman slips off her robe/housecoat – this can be done offstage.)

(The middle-aged woman then appears in a black suit and the younger woman appears in a black sleeveless dress.)

VOICE OFFSTAGE. Are you ready? It's almost time to go.

BOTH WOMEN. I'll be right there.

(They then exit the stage and we hear...)

TV VOICE. The death of yet another unarmed Black man has sparked days of protests. But today instead of focusing on how he died, the focus is on celebrating how he lived and the remarkable life of a young man who is gone far too soon. His mother and wife, are both scheduled to speak at his memorial which we will be carrying live shortly.

> *(We then see the two women come together in the front of the stage, holding hands, and then embracing, in tears.)*

> *(Lights down.)*

17. The Ball

(Before lights come back up we either see a television flickering, or imagery denoting a television is on somewhere. As lights come up we then hear the TV VOICE below begin.)

TV VOICE. Thousands of activists are expected to clash amidst organized protests in Washington D.C., but also nationwide.

(Lights up on a hair salon. One lady is seated under a hairdryer, another is seated in a salon chair where her hair is being done by the third lady. There is a photo of Whitney Houston with an elegant updo taped to the mirror.)

SHANIECE. Could you turn that down?

RENITA. Sure thing, hon.

(The TV VOICE goes off.)

SHANIECE. I just...

RENITA. I know. Today is a special day and you want to...

SHANIECE. I just want a day to focus on the good, not the bad for a change and we all finally have some good to focus on.

RENITA. Sure do! And don't you worry, when I finish with you, you're going to look just like a princess.

SHANIECE. I want to look like a queen.

RENITA. Alright then, Miss Queen.

(Pause.)

SHANIECE. You spoken to her yet?

RENITA. No. Cause I have nothing to say. I said everything I had to say the other day and she got an attitude. *(Pause.)* I tried to tell her.

SHANIECE. You know she never listens to nobody.

BRENDA. Tell who what?

RENITA. Stop sticking your head out from under that dryer or it's never gonna dry!

BRENDA. I can't hear!

RENITA. We're not talking about you so you don't need to hear.

> *(She goes back under the dryer... They wait a beat.)*

What do you think she's gonna do?

SHANIECE. Nothin. Like she always does.

RENITA. Nothin!? Nothin?!? She needs to put him out.

BRENDA. Put who out?

> *(RENITA glares at BRENDA who pouts and goes back under the dryer...)*

SHANIECE. The lease is in his name and they cut back her hours at the plant. So she said she can't afford to leave right now.

RENITA. I tried to tell her.

SHANIECE. I know. We all did.

RENITA. When are you all going to learn?

SHANIECE. Oh here we go...

RENITA. Well it's the truth. I know you better than your mamas do. I know you better than your doctors do.

> *(SHANIECE laughs.)*

Laugh all you want to but who did you tell you were pregnant first?

SHANIECE. I didn't tell you. You guessed.

RENITA. Same difference. And who told you to marry Sam?

SHANIECE. You did.

RENITA. And who told you NOT to marry Eddie, because he's a player?

SHANIECE. You did.

RENITA. And who's currently cheating on your poor cousin right now?

SHANIECE. Eddie.

BRENDA. Freddie's cheating?

RENITA. Girl – if you don't keep your behind UNDER that dryer and out of our business!!

(**BRENDA** *goes back under the dryer...*)

How much does she need?

SHANIECE. What?

RENITA. How much does she need to move?

SHANIECE. No! No. That's not why I told you...

RENITA. I know it's not. And I didn't ask why you told me. I asked you how much she needs.

SHANIECE. I don't know. She doesn't like to ask for help.

RENITA. She didn't ask. But I'm offering. You have her come by here. I'll do her hair – for free – and we'll figure it out.

SHANIECE. We can't let you do that.

RENITA. You're not letting me do anything. First off, it's my money and I will do with it as I see fit and right now

I see fit to help her move out and move on from that triflin,' no good –

BRENDA. Ohhhh – ya'll must be talkin' about Eddie, not Freddie.

RENITA. Girl!

SHANIECE. Well she's not wrong. I wonder how many women in this shop would know we were talkin' about him just by that description, cause he is a triflin,' no good...

(**RENITA** *glares at* **BRENDA.**)

BRENDA. I know! I know. (*Mimicking* **RENITA.**) "Brenda, get your behind back under that dryer."

RENITA. You keep messin' around and you're going find yourself finishing your hair, yourself, somewhere else.

(**BRENDA** *goes back under the dryer.*)

Where was I?

SHANIECE. Talkin' about my cousin's no good, triflin' ...

RENITA. Right! Eddie. Second: I'm grown, and I will spend my money helping whoever I want to. Third: how long have ya'll been coming here?

SHANIECE. I don't know. Long as I can remember. Maybe seven, eight years old?

RENITA. Somewhere around there – and even when you were small you were better at sitting under the dryer like you were supposed to than she is.

(*They look at* **BRENDA** *who can't hear but just waves at them cluelessly... they wave back.*)

You girls are family and family takes care of each other. So you tell your cousin, whatever she needs – I got her.

(If they can't hug because of the chair. They hold hands in a way that "family" does...)

How's your mama doing?

SHANIECE. Not great. But she's excited about tonight. She wants me to bring her lots of pictures.

RENITA. And bring me some too. I'm so excited you'd think I was going.

(Pause.)

Sam going with you?

SHANIECE. No he has to work. It's a good week to be a security guard.

RENITA. He's always been a hard worker.

SHANIECE. I know. You told me that when you first told me I should let him take me out. You remember?

RENITA. How could I forget? You had seen that model who shaved part of her head and left the other side long.

SHANIECE. Don't remind me.

RENITA. I tried to tell you not to follow some model but you insisted and when I wouldn't do it, you went to what's her name...

SHANIECE. Shauntay.

RENITA. Shauntay... who isn't even a real stylist...

SHANIECE. How many more times are you going to bring this up?

RENITA. You brought it up.

SHANIECE. I brought up my husband. You're the one bringing up ancient hair history.

RENITA. That's because he had seen your picture before you went and messed up your hair and you didn't want to go out with him because you were afraid your hair looked a mess. And it did. And then you called me, like you were calling 911 in the middle of a natural disaster.

SHANIECE. Well my hair was a disaster. And I did apologize for letting someone else do my hair for the first – and last – time in my life. And I do believe that was the first of like one hundred apologies.

RENITA. And I accepted your apology and...

SHANIECE. And you fixed it up. And then I went out with him... and the rest is history.

BRENDA. That's a real beautiful story.

> (**BRENDA** *has popped her head out from under the dryer. She sees* **RENITA**'s *face and goes back under the dryer.*)

I know. I know. (*Mimicking* **RENITA**.) "Girl if you don't get your head back under that dryer!"

> (*She then goes back under the dryer.*)

RENITA. Ya'll had one of the prettiest weddings I've ever seen. And I'm gonna brag a little. I know I'm good, but I do believe I outdid myself that day. Your hair was fierce! (*She snaps at the fierceness of it all.*)

SHANIECE. Sam did say I was the most beautiful bride in the history of brides.

RENITA. Well he would say that because he loves you. That man thinks you walk on water. But I have to say I been to a lot of weddings, and I think he might be right.

SHANIECE. You're sweet.

RENITA. Telling the truth. Between your hair, your makeup, your dress... you looked like a movie star. Glamorous and classy. I was so proud of you. I always knew you'd make something of yourself. Grow up and have a nice life. And here you are, grown, graduated and married and going to fancy events. Lord, I'm so proud you'd think I actually brought you into this world.

SHANIECE. Renita, you said it yourself, we are as much family as anyone connected by blood. How many times did I come and sit in one of these chairs crying and pouring my heart out about some boy who broke my heart who mama didn't even know I was dating.

RENITA. Yeah and I'm still looking for that little jackass Dwayne, standing you up for prom. If I ever see him, he's in trouble.

SHANIECE. That was twenty years ago.

RENITA. It's never too late for a man to learn some manners and never too late for me to teach him some.

SHANIECE. Well, even though I didn't actually get to go that night – my hair looked fly. You made sure of that.

RENITA. Main reason I'm mad at Dwayne. I never got to see that pretty prom picture of you all done up in your hair and dress that night with your corsage. Ooh – what's your dress for tonight look like?

SHANIECE. It's red. It's strapless.

RENITA. Sounds sexy. You got a picture?

SHANIECE. Yeah.

(*She pulls out her phone.*)

RENITA. Oooohhh that's niiiice...

(*We see* **BRENDA** *looking forlorn.*)

Please pass her that phone before she starts crying.

(**SHANIECE** *passes* **BRENDA** *her phone.* **BRENDA** *lifts up the hair dryer and says...*)

BRENDA. Ooooh! That's nice!

RENITA. Now I see why you gave me that old picture of Whitney Houston at the Grammys. You're going to look even more glamorous than her between your hair and that dress. You WILL look like a Queen.

SHANIECE. You think so?

RENITA. I KNOW SO.

SHANIECE. I'm a little... nervous.

RENITA. Nervous? Why? Pretty girl like you? Nights like this make me wish I was your age again.

SHANIECE. I don't know. I'm not used to going to stuff like this and being around all those bougie people and fancy folks.

RENITA. You belong at that ball just as much as anybody else, and frankly with THAT dress and THIS hair you're going to steal the show.

(SHANIECE *giggles.*)

That was real nice of your boss to give you that ticket.

SHANIECE. Oh, it wasn't my boss. It was Sam's. Even though he couldn't go he wanted me to have it. Told me to have fun playing Cinderella.

RENITA. You got yourself a good man.

SHANIECE. I know. And I've always known that and been so proud of him. But I gotta say – I feel like the last few weeks, he's held his head up a little higher. You know? Walked a little taller. I feel like him, his brothers, his friends... they're all good men. They've always been good men. But now, it's like there's this extra pride that they have... you know?

RENITA. Yeah, honey. I know. We all have it today.

BRENDA. Hey!

RENITA. You're not dry!

(Before **RENITA** *can say anything else...)*

BRENDA. It's almost time! Turn it up.

RENITA. *(Looks at the time.)* Oh you're right!

*(**RENITA** goes to turn the TV sound up...)*

(To **BRENDA.***)* Turn your dryer off so we can hear.

VOICE FROM THE TV SCREEN. Senator Barack Obama and his wife, Michelle, have arrived. Soon he will make history when he is sworn in as the 44th President of the United States.

(Lights down.)

18. Pauline on When Hair Gets Political

(**PAULINE,** *a Congresswoman, is giving an interview. We never see the* **REPORTER.***)*

You know it's funny. The first time I was asked if I thought the fact that I wear my hair in locks would hurt my chances of being elected President I wasn't trying to be funny when I replied, "Have you seen Donald Trump's hair?"

I'm serious. Have you?

I think voters have a lot more on their minds than what a candidate's hair looks like. In my whole career, first in the City Council then in Congress, I've gotten close to fifteen thousand letters – most of them form letters and emails, telling me to vote for or against a piece of legislation. But I've gotten maybe one hundred letters about my hair. And thirty came from a Girl Scout Troop telling me how much they liked my hair. Was so cute. Of course there have been a few critics mixed in, but the truth is I've gotten way more letters about my glasses. Apparently people have strong feelings about the color. Some think the red frames make me look like a Black Sally Jesse Raphael.

To which I say, "What's wrong with that?"

Wait – how old are you?

(Pause.)

Well google Sally Jesse Raphael.

The point is I just don't have too much time to worry about what they say about my looks. It's not why I ran for office. I ran for office the first time because someone needed to do something. A friend from high school, her son was shot and killed. Great kid. Just in the wrong place. Everyone says if you just do the right thing – go to school, stay out of trouble – you'll be fine. But that's a lie. I told my friend *she* should run for office. But she didn't. She couldn't. Like a lot of women who decline to run, she had too many people in her life who depended on her, including a sick mom she was caring for. So I'm here. And I keep the same picture on my desk in my campaign office, that was on my desk in my city council office and on my desk in Washington of her and her son.

She doesn't care what my hair looks like. So I don't.

Obviously I know as a person in the public eye how I look matters some. And being a woman it probably matters more than it would if I were a guy. When Hillary Clinton pointed out that she had to wake up earlier than all of the men she was running against for President, because of the extra ninety minutes she had to spend every day getting hair and makeup ready, she wasn't lying. I may not choose to be defined by my looks, but I'm not an idiot. Most women candidates don't feel like we can go on camera makeup free but maybe a generation from now a female candidate will sit here saying she feels about makeup the way I feel about hair. But ultimately, I try not to let what's on my head rent too much space in my head.

Over the years, I've gotten letters from other Black women sharing their stories of the opportunities they've lost because of their hair. So that's why I helped pass a bill when I was working in the City Council targeting hair discrimination. We still have a long way to go, though. New York banned discrimination on the basis of hair in schools, public places and workplaces. It became statewide law in 2019 and that same year California passed the Crown Act which stands for "Create a Respectful and Open Workplace for Natural Hair" and other states are trying to pass similar laws to protect us too. So I'm feeling really hopeful.

And I want to be clear. These bills are not just about getting white people to lighten up... well maybe that's a poor choice of words, but you know what I mean. One of the things I learned is that this baggage we carry around when it comes to hair, it weighs down all of us... collectively as a society. It weighs us down by... wasting our time, our energy our productivity and yes it wounds people in ways some people may never recover from...

My friend Ally Bankston, said that years ago at her very first job out of law school an older Black female partner actually reprimanded her for wearing her hair in braids at the office on a Saturday and Ally ended up being pressured to leave the firm. She obviously got the last laugh because now she's a Congresswoman and her old firm recently hosted a fundraiser for her. But how sad is it that another Black woman felt Ally, one of the smartest women I know, was some kind of embarrassment to her – to all of us – because of her hair.

But you know when Chirlane McCray, became the First Lady of New York City a few years ago, she had dreads and it was hardly talked about, and I don't remember reading any handwringing op-eds about Lori Lightfoot having natural hair, when she became the first Black female mayor of Chicago. And Congresswoman Karen Bass wears her hair natural and that hardly came up when her name was floated as a possible vice-presidential contender. These women are proof that we're making progress and things *are* getting better. I mean I think it's worth noting that the one time President Trump tweeted about me, he tweeted about my comments on immigration, not my hair. I think that's a good thing. We should be talking about the issues, not the stuff that doesn't really matter.

But I know that representation DOES matter. I know there are little Black boys who believe they can be President someday because they got to see Barack

Obama and there are little brown girls who now know they can be Vice President because of Kamala Harris. So if some teenager with locks believes she has a better shot at becoming a Member of Congress or President because of me, I embrace it.

I'm certainly proud of the bills I've written, and even prouder of the bills I've passed, but at the end of the day it's not just about the laws that we pass but the legacy we're leaving behind. For Black people the story we've been told about ourselves is not a very pretty one. So that's really the work I'm doing every day and other women and men in positions like mine are doing every day. We are trying to rewrite a history that either left us out all together or tried to diminish us, our contributions our cultural norms, and even how we look.

The fact that there are little Black girls who don't think they're beautiful because of their hair or their features – that comes from society telling their moms, their dads and their grandparents that, and that being passed down through the generations. So the real work is making sure that the next generation can hold their heads up a little higher and walk a little taller than we did.

> *(Images displayed on a screen, or represented visually in some other capacity, should show black women trailblazers from the world of politics who represent hair diversity, such as Rep. Karen Bass, Shirley Chisolm, Vice President Kamala Harris, Barbara Jordan, Mayor Lori Lightfoot and Chirlane McCray.*)*

> *(Lights down.)*

---

* A license to produce THE GLORIOUS WORLD OF CROWNS, KINKS AND CURLS does not include a license to publicly display any third-party or copyrighted images. Licensees must acquire rights for any copyrighted images or create their own.

19. Dear God, It's Me, Claire

(This scene should serve as a mirror/echo to the earlier scene "Dear God, It's Me, Amaya." Only this time the year that is denoted on stage is 2019.)

Dear God...

It's me Claire. I know you know that. Mommy says you know everything. If that's true then you know she's being REALLY unfair for grounding me.

It's not my fault that Shane Dalton has a bloody nose.

(Pause.)

I mean, yes I hit him.

But only after he called us ugly.

If he hadn't called us ugly. I wouldn't have hit him and then he wouldn't have a bloody nose.

So please help mommy understand this and please help make Shane less dumb.

Mommy said Shane has been in-doctor... in-a-doctor... in...

Hold on let me grab my notebook... I wrote it down...

(Pause.)

Shane has been indoctri-nated to believe in... to believe in... hold on I wrote it down.

(Pause.)

EURO-PEEING beauty standards.

So he thinks you have to have light skin and long hair to be pretty which is like... the dumbest thing I've ever heard. I mean Miss Universe is officially the prettiest girl in the world... in the whole universe and she has dark skin and short hair.

> *(The image of Miss Universe Zozibini Tuni should appear.*)*

She's from Africa. But since she's Miss Universe every girl in the entire Universe gets to claim her, including me.

Mommy said when she was growing up she sometimes felt ugly because back then people made her feel like being brown with our kind of hair is ugly. But I KNOW I'm NOT ugly... I mean just look at me. You did SUCH a good job, making me, God. Congratulations.

I know other little girls are cute but daddy says I'm beautiful and my daddy is the smartest man in the world.

Also, I know I'm beautiful because I look like Miss Universe. I'm brown and I have hair like hers and Miss Universe *is* the most beautiful lady ever. Next to mommy of course.

So Shane is just plain stupid. I know this, but my friend Keisha... well what Shane said made her cry. That's why I hit him.

Keisha's the darkest one in her family and doesn't look like her mom. I mean she does, but her mom has longer hair and is more tan. But my mommy always says beauty comes in different shapes and sizes and colors. But I don't think Keisha believes that.

Speaking of my mom, God, can you make sure she knows that Shane deserved it? Mommy's name is Amaya – I mean I know you probably know that

---

* A license to produce THE GLORIOUS WORLD OF CROWNS, KINKS AND CURLS does not include a license to publicly display any third-party or copyrighted images. Licensees must acquire rights for any copyrighted images or create their own.

– but you probably have lots of kids in trouble who are praying to you right now so I'm just trying to help. My mom's name is AMAYA *(Over enunciating for effect.)* And please let her know I was right. Shane was wrong and I shouldn't be in trouble.

(We hear **HER MOTHER**'s *voice offstage...)*

HER MOTHER. Claire – let's go.

CLAIRE. Coming mommy!

Oh-- and since you know everything God... *(She begins to whisper...)*

I know you know I took those two cookies and then blamed my little brother. And I know that was wrong, but since he's only two years old, mommy and daddy think everything he does is cute so they won't ground him and I think you and I can both agree that...

(Pause.)

Well... I just really don't want to be grounded... but I know it was wrong and I'm sorry...

*(***HER MOTHER*** again...)*

HER MOTHER. Claire!!!!

CLAIRE. Coming mommy!

Amen!

(Lights down.)

20. Scars

(One of the **LADIES** *who did not portray the* **ACTRESS** *in the opening scene is on stage when the lights come up. She has extremely curly hair. A* **CASTING DIRECTOR**'s *voice can be heard, but as a callback/mirror to the opening scene, we can't see her... at first.)*

YOUNGER ACTRESS. ... So I graduated from Tisch in May and I've been really fortunate to do some readings for some really great writers...

(Pause.)

But I've mainly been waiting tables.

CASTING DIRECTOR/THE ORIGINAL ACTRESS. No shame in that.

YOUNGER ACTRESS. I also just filmed my TV debut. Hasn't aired yet.

CASTING DIRECTOR/THE ORIGINAL ACTRESS. Great. What's the show?

YOUNGER ACTRESS. It's the newest *Law & Order* franchise.

CASTING DIRECTOR/THE ORIGINAL ACTRESS. That's awesome. Good for you. Tell me about your character.

(Long pause.)

YOUNGER ACTRESS. Umm... I'm... the corpse they find in the opening scene.

CASTING DIRECTOR/ORIGINAL ACTRESS. Well, we all gotta start somewhere. *(Pause.)*

Thanks for coming in.

YOUNGER ACTRESS. Thanks for seeing me.

> *(She turns to go. Then turns back.)*

Listen, I know every actress says this, but I really, really, really love this play. And I'd give my right arm to be in it – even to just play a corpse. For the record, the director of my *Law & Order* episode said I was the most convincing corpse he'd seen in a really long time.

Seriously, I love this play and these characters so much that if you all need me to change up my appearance or anything to fit with the look of the play, I'm happy to do that.

CASTING DIRECTOR/ORIGINAL ACTRESS. Change your appearance?

YOUNGER ACTRESS. Yeah. I know my hair looks a little wacky today, but my agent called at the last minute and said you guys could squeeze me in. So I literally raced from the restaurant to get here. But I want you to know that I can straighten my hair or do whatever you all need me to. I saw the Broadway production of *Scars* when I was in high school, so I know none of the actresses in the main roles have hair like mine, so I can change it. I can get it pressed or relaxed or whatever. Heck – I'll even shave it off if you need me to.

CASTING DIRECTOR/ORIGINAL ACTRESS. That won't be necessary.

> *(At that the **CASTING DIRECTOR** joins her on stage and we see it is the **ACTRESS** from the opening scene and "It's Just Hair".)*

Your hair is fabulous. And I started my own theater company so that an actress with your talent wouldn't ever have to decide between doing that to her hair or playing a role that she was born to play. So, I'll see you at the callback. But promise me one thing.

YOUNGER ACTRESS. Sure. Anything.

CASTING DIRECTOR/ORIGINAL ACTRESS. Don't touch your hair.

End of Play